THE DREAM BIRD

THE DREAM BIRD

Written by

Lale Süphandağı

Published by Tughra Books
345 Clifton Ave., Clifton,
NJ, 07011, USA

www.tughrabooks.com

THE DREAM BIRD
Project Editor: Betül Ertekin
Translated by Hülya Arınık and Emine Acar
Graphic Design: İbrahim Akdağ

ISBN: 978-1-59784-282-2

Printed by
Çağlayan A.S. Izmir, Turkey

CONTENTS

Dear Parents,

In our daily lives we read many books so as to know the Prophets, peace be upon them, better. We try to relay all that we have learnt from these books to our children. However, it is of utmost importance to be able to give information at a level that pre-school children can understand. That is why we have prepared this book about the lives of the Prophets, taking into account the developmental stages and the imagination of preschoolers. We bestow these wonderful stories to all children.

OUR BELOVED
PROPHET

Shakir prayed again that night before he went to bed. He wanted to see our Prophet, peace and blessings be upon him, in his dream so much. As soon as he closed his eyes, he found himself in the land of dreams. At that moment, the Dream Bird came to him.

Excitedly Shakir said:

"Oh Dream Bird! How did I get here?"

"Tonight you are my guest. I heard that you loved our Prophet and wished to see him in your dream," explained the Dream Bird.

"Yes, I want that very much," answered Shakir.

9

"In that case, are you ready for the journey?" asked the Dream Bird.

"Yes, I'm ready!" said Shakir.

"Now I will take you to the night our Prophet was born," the Dream Bird said smiling.

Excitedly, Shakir jumped on the back of the Dream Bird. Shakir was very happy as he was flying up high! Suddenly, the Dream Bird pointed to a shining star and said:

"Shakir, the name of that shining star is Sirius. It bears the good news that our Prophet was just born."

Shakir couldn't believe his ears.

Moments later they came to a shining house. The Dream Bird said:

"Look, this is the house our Prophet was born in."

Shakir said: "Oh, this house is shining!"

The Dream Bird smiled and said:

"That light you see is the radiance of our Prophet. And the rosy smell that radiates is his beautiful scent."

Shakir said: "Yes! It is a beautiful smell."

Then, the Dream Bird asked Shakir curiously:

"I wonder if you know the name of our Prophet?"

"Of course I know! His name is Muhammad, the Messenger of Allah," answered Shakir.

"Good for you Shakir," said the Dream Bird.

Soon after, the skies were brightened with the first rays of the sun. The Dream Bird continued to fly. Soon they came to a very crowded bazaar.

Shakir asked in surprise: "Why is it so crowded here?"

The Dream Bird said: "There have been blessings and abundance everywhere because our Prophet was born. Lots and lots of fruits and vegetables are sold at the markets now.

Then the Dream Bird told Shakir to close his eyes. When Shakir opened his eyes, he saw that they had come to a high hill. There were lambs grazing on it.

Shakir said: "These lambs are very cute."

The Dream Bird replied: "Our Prophet lived here when he was a baby. Halima suckled and cared for him."

Shakir listened to the Dream Bird carefully.

Suddenly the Dream Bird started to beat his wings quickly. Where were they going now? After passing some hills the Dream Bird said:

"Here look! That building you see in the shape of a black box is the Ka'ba."

Shakir curiously asked: "What is the Ka'ba?"

"The Ka'ba is the first holy place where Muslims started to pray to Allah. The Ka'ba is very important for all Muslims," explained the Dream Bird.

After a while he looked at Shakir and said: "Now I will take you to a different time."

Flying through the clouds they came to the place where there were tall date trees.

The Dream Bird said: "Shakir, look! We have come to the beautiful city of Medina."

18

When they looked down below, they saw a huge crowd. The people there were either carrying stones or water. As they came closer, Shakir saw someone whose face was bright like the moon. He tried to understand what was happening. He rubbed his eyes. The Dream Bird pointed at someone with his wing and asked:

"Do you see the Prophet?"

Shakir said in surprise: "You mean our Prophet? Oh, he is so handsome."

Dream bird explained, "He is helping his friends build Al-Masjid an-Nabawi, the Prophet's Mosque.

Shakir still could not believe his eyes. With great excitement he said: "My dear Prophet! I love you very much."

Shakir continued to fly swiftly through the clouds with the Dream Bird. Moments later they stopped at the peak of the Jabal an-Nur, the Mountain of Light. The Dream Bird said:

"It is here that Allah began to give the verses of our Holy Book, the Qur'an to our Prophet. Later our Prophet introduced the Qur'an to everybody else. He was an example to everybody around him with his great behavior. We all love him very much."

The Dream Bird continued:

"Shakir, our journey with you has been wonderful. Other children are waiting for me in the world of dreams. I need to go."

Shakir hugged the Dream Bird and said: "I had a wonderful journey. Thank you very much Dream Bird" and then he thanked Allah.

When Shakir woke up he felt very happy.

He raised his hands and said:

"Dear Allah, I love our Prophet. Insha'Allah, I will see him in my dream again."

Then he ran to his mother and father because he couldn't wait to tell them about his wonderful dream.

THE TALKING BABY

Marwa loves her new-born brother. She cares for him each day and says, "I wish he could talk to me." She always goes to sleep and gets up early. One night, she felt asleep immediately after she went to bed and found herself in the land of dreams.

25

The Dream Bird was smiling and standing right in front of the little girl.

"Dream Bird, why did you come into my dream?" Marwa asked.

"Didn't you make a wish that babies could talk?" the Dream Bird said.

"Yes," said Marwa in amazement.

"Then, I am going to take you on a journey through time! Are you ready?" the Dream Bird asked.

"Yes, I'm ready!" cried Marwa.

Marwa hopped onto the Dream Bird's back. They started flying high in the sky through the colorful clouds that looked like puffs of cotton.

Marwa was a little bit scared to fly at first. Then she realized that this journey was so much fun.

A little while later, the Dream Bird started to descend all of a sudden, and said:

"Marwa, do you see that mother with a child in her arms? Her name is Maryam (Mary). Despite the difficulties throughout her life, she always loved Allah very much and always prayed to Him."

"I love Allah very much and I always pray to Him too," Marwa exclaimed."

"Good for you, Marwa! Now let's go over and listen to what she is saying," said the Dream Bird.

As they got closer, they realized that Maryam was talking to the people around her.

The people asked:

"Maryam! Who is that child? What is he doing in your arms?"

Maryam then pointed to the baby.

Everyone looked in amazement. A baby can't talk! Then right at that moment, the miracle baby raised his hand and said:

"Without a doubt, I am a servant of Allah. Allah gave me a book and made me a Prophet. He ordered me to be kind to my mother."

Nobody had ever seen or heard anything like this before. This was a great miracle from Allah. The talking baby was Allah's Prophet Isa (Jesus), peace be upon him. Marwa listened very carefully to what was being said.

"Marwa, you look shocked at what you have seen," the Dream Bird said.

"Yes, very much," she replied.

"Now close your eyes. We are going to travel to another time," said the Dream Bird.

Marwa was so excited. She closed her eyes right away.

When she opened her eyes she saw people sitting on the floor around a dinner table.

"Look Marwa! Do you see this table with so many different kinds of food on it? These people have just asked Prophet Isa to bring down a feast from the skies. Prophet Isa prayed to Allah. Allah commanded His angels to bring down this food," said the Dream Bird.

Marwa opened her eyes wide.

"Oh, really?" she exclaimed.

"Yes," said the Dream Bird. "Right now they're eating this wonderful food and giving thanks to Allah."

After that, the Dream Bird started flying back up towards the sky. A short time later they heard an old man cry out:

"Thanks be to my Allah. Thanks be to my Allah!"

Marwa asked why the man was screaming.

The Dream Bird smiled and said:

"Because just now Prophet Isa touched this blind man's eyes with his hands. The man hadn't been able to see anything for years, and now, miraculously, he can see!"

Marwa was both very happy and very amazed.

After that, the Dream Bird took Marwa to a riverbank. While Marwa watched and listened to the sparkling water, the Dream Bird continued:

"Prophet Isa always healed the people who were sick. This was one of his miracles. Did you know that Prophet Isa also gave the news that our Prophet Muhammad was going to come after him as the last Prophet?"

The Dream Bird then started flapping his bright and shiny wings and said:

"Dear Marwa, our journey through time has come to an end."

Marwa kissed the Dream Bird and said, "Our journey together was amazing. I even got to know a Prophet. I wish it had never ended."

When she woke up, her heart was beating quickly. She was excited to have such an amazing dream. She looked at the sky through the window of her room and said, "I hope we travel with the Dream Bird again."

38

THE PROPHET WITH A STAFF

Umar and his parents went to the village of his grandfather. The beautiful house of his grandfather was beside a river. Umar watched some small pieces of wood floating on the river. Suddenly, one of the pieces began to drift away. He followed it downstream.

It was a tiring day and Umar wanted to get some rest. He sat under a tall tree with big leaves and fell asleep.

The Dream Bird came to his dream.

"Hello Umar. Are you ready for a long trip with me?" the Dream Bird asked.

"Sure, I am. Where are we going?" replied Umar.

"Far away, to a baby in a basket floating on a river," said the Dream Bird.

Umar was both surprised and happy. Then the Dream Bird helped Umar to get on his back by spreading out his wings.

They began to fly up high. There was a warm wind flowing in the sky. Umar had never been so happy before.

43

After a while they came to a long river.

Then Umar noticed something. A woman was running to the river while carrying her baby in her arms. The Dream Bird, seeing Umar was curious said, "She is the mother of Musa (Moses), peace be upon him. She is going to put the baby in the Nile River in a basket."

"Really, why?" asked Umar.

"Because the Pharaoh, the king of the country, had a dream. He told his dream to some fortune-tellers. They said that a baby was going to be born soon and when that baby grew up, he was going to destroy this kingdom. So he ordered every boy baby should be killed at birth. The mother of Musa was very worried, and prepared a basket as Allah commanded her.

45

She is going to put him in the basket and place it on the river, so that the soldiers of the Pharaoh will not find him," said the Dream Bird.

"Look, Dream Bird! She put the baby in the basket, and placed it in the river," cried out Umar with excitement.

"The basket has already begun to float on the river. Let's follow it," said the Dream Bird.

After a while, the drifting basket stopped near the palace. The servants were very surprised to see a baby in the basket, and immediately took him to the palace.

47

"Oh, what is going to happen now?" asked Umar.

"They are going to take him to Asiya, the wife of the Pharaoh. Let's go to the window of the palace and take a look," said the Dream Bird.

Umar looked through the window with interest. Asiya was very happy seeing the baby. What a beautiful baby he was. She immediately went to her husband.

"We cannot see them. What is going to happen now?" asked Umar.

"She is going to convince the Pharaoh to keep the baby. Musa is going to be raised in the palace. Umar, close your eyes now. We are going to a new time," said the Dream Bird.

After a short trip, they stopped on a high mountain.

"The Prophet Musa spoke to Allah on this mountain. He was chosen as a Prophet. The Holy Book Tawrat (Torah) was given to him here. The Prophet Musa showed a lot of miracles through his staff, by the help of Allah," said the Dream Bird.

"How nice! I am very glad to meet Prophet Musa," said Umar.

Then the Dream Bird began to fly again, and they were above a big sea. He was very surprised. Everything was so big and amazing.

"Look, the sea is split into two parts. And now people are walking in between!" said Umar.

"A short time ago, Musa hit the sea with his staff, and the sea split into two parts, by the permission of Allah. That's because they needed to escape from the soldiers of Pharaoh by, going to the opposite shore," said the Dream Bird.

"What if they catch them!" said Umar worriedly.

"Don't worry Umar! They are going to cross through the sea until the soldiers come, by the permission of Allah," said the Dream Bird.

Then they began to fly again.

"Dear Umar, it is now the end of our trip," said the Dream Bird.

53

Umar was in amazement when he woke up. His grandfather was smiling and looking at him.

"We were looking for you. Then we saw you asleep under this tree," said his grandfather.

"Grandpa I had a very beautiful dream," said Umar. He told his dream to his grandfather as they walked back to the house.

54